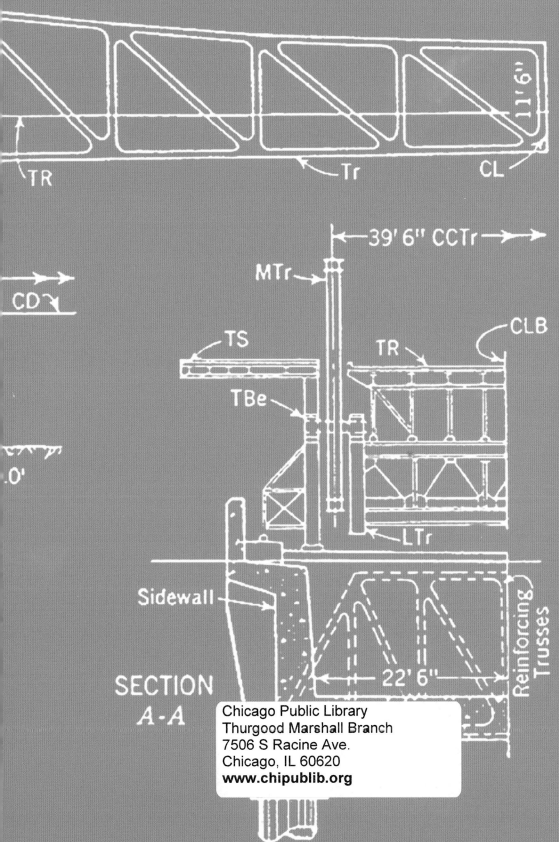

11'6"

TR

Tr

CL

39'6" CCTr

MTr

CD

TS

TR

CLB

TBe

LTr

Sidewall

Reinforcing Trusses

22'6"

SECTION
A-A

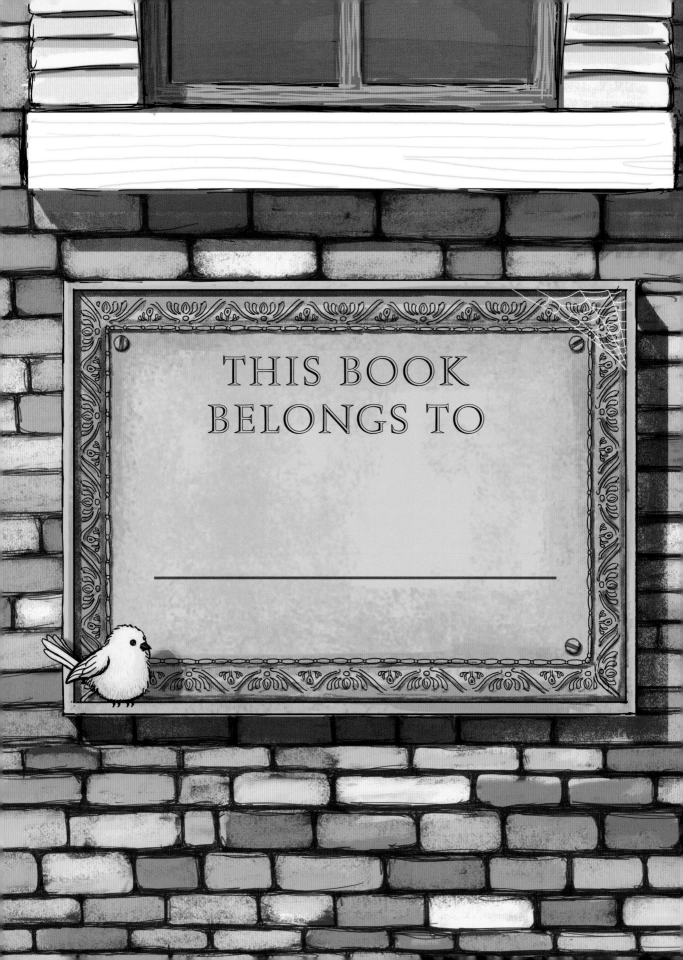

THIS BOOK
BELONGS TO

_____

DRAWBRIDGES
Open and Close

PTM
Werks Series

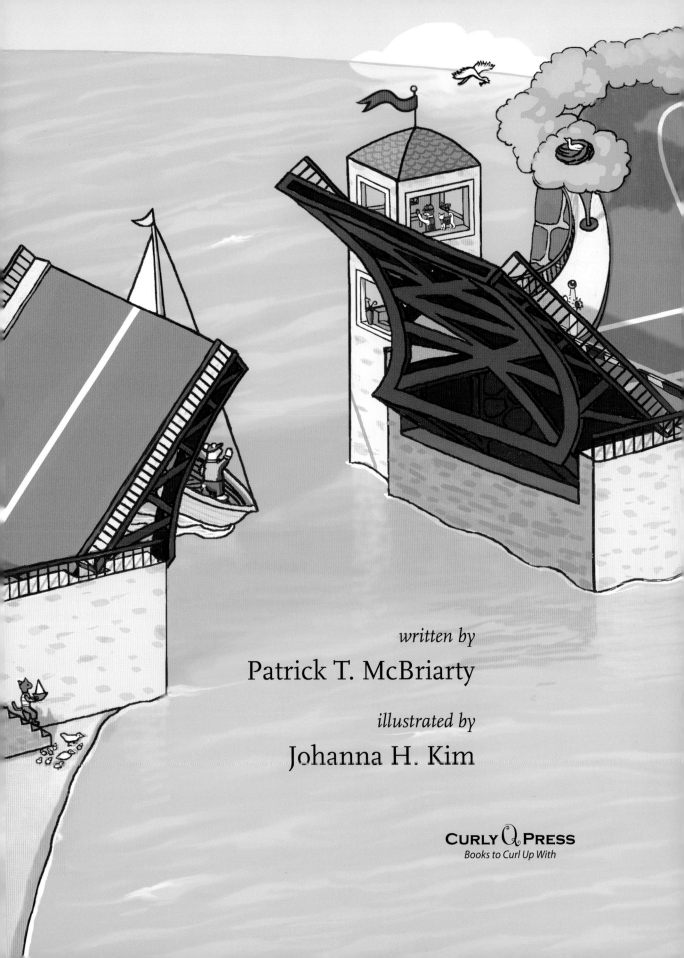

written by

Patrick T. McBriarty

illustrated by

Johanna H. Kim

CURLY Q PRESS
Books to Curl Up With

Next to the drawbridge is a bridge house.

Inside are the controls and underneath are the bridge motors and gears. This is where Bridge Tender Todd works.

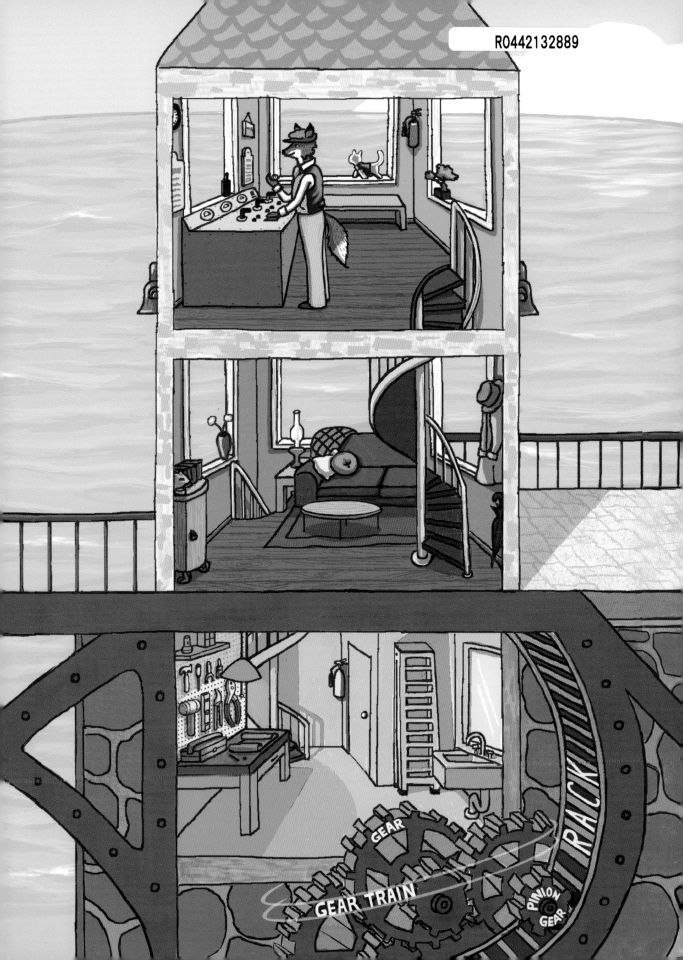

GEAR

GEAR TRAIN

RACK

PINION GEAR

In the distance, a tugboat towing a big barge
chug-chug-chugs toward the drawbridge.

Captain Josie Kangaroo pulls a cord in her tugboat. *Toot TOOT!* sings the tugboat towing the big barge.

She calls on the radio, "Please (CRACKLE) open the drawbridge (CRACKLE). Over."

From the top floor of the bridge house Bridge Tender Todd operates the controls to open and close the drawbridge. His sidekick Ponticat is also there to help out.

"Roger, will do!" (*CRACKLE*) "Over and out," says Bridge Tender Todd into his radio.

BELLS AND LIGHTS. Bridge Tender Todd turns the first switch. *Clang-clang! Flash-flash.* The warning bells and lights let everyone know the bridge is about to open.

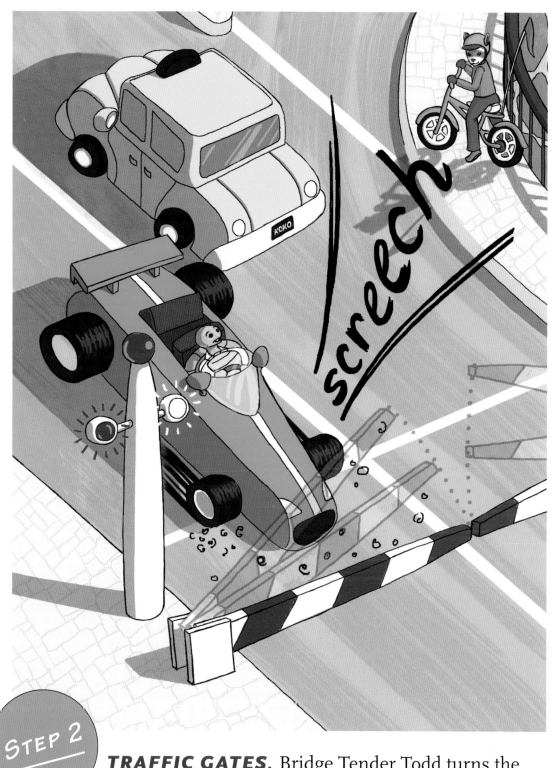

STEP 2

TRAFFIC GATES. Bridge Tender Todd turns the second switch. The traffic gates go down, down, down bringing street traffic to a stop.

STEP 3

CHECK THE BRIDGE.
Bridge Tender Todd looks outside to make sure everything is "A-OK."

STEP 4

UNLOCK THE BRIDGE. Bridge Tender Todd turns the third switch.

Motors hum and metal scrapes, as the drawbridge is unlocked and ready to lift.

STEP 5

DOUBLE CHECK. Always careful, Bridge Tender Todd looks outside to make sure everyone and everything is off the bridge and "A-OK."

STEP 6

OPEN THE BRIDGE. Bridge Tender Todd eases the big lever back. *Click-brrr-click.*

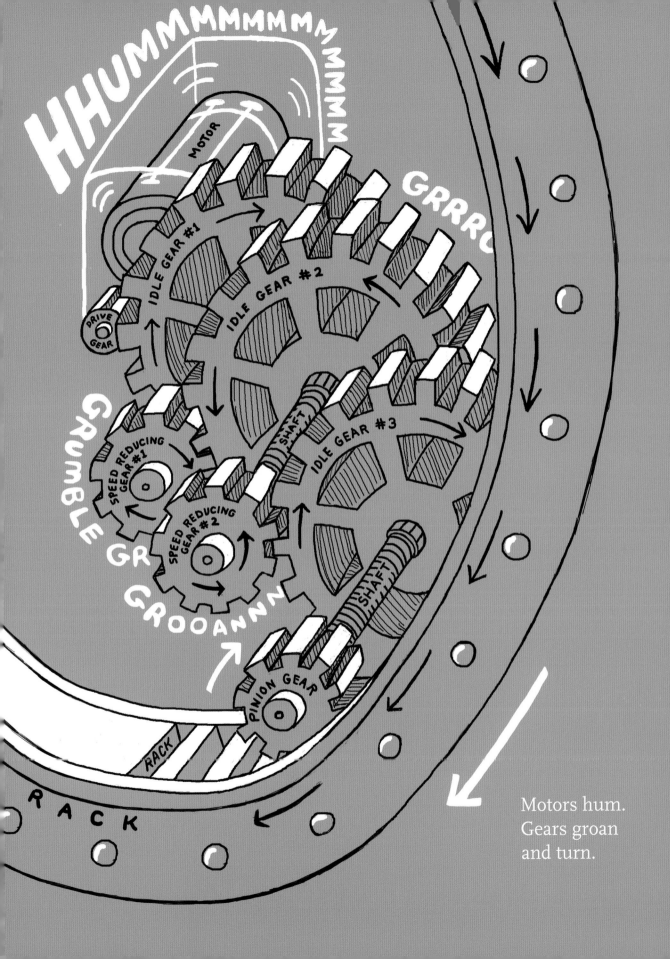

Motors hum.
Gears groan
and turn.

Clang-clang, flash-flash. With the hum of motors, gears spin and whir, and slowly the bridge rises. . .

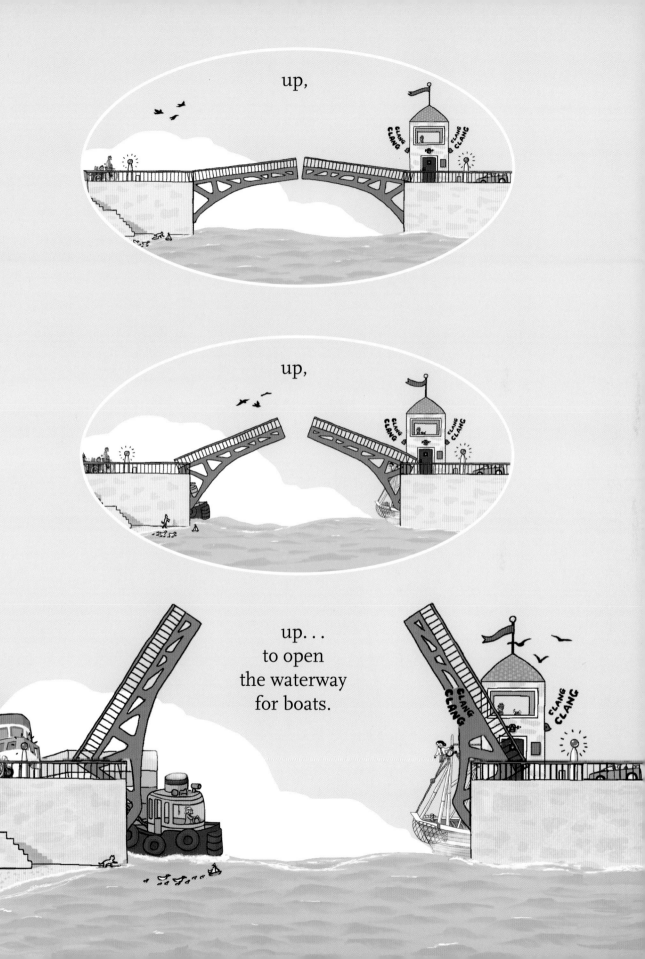

up,

up,

up...
to open
the waterway
for boats.

funky fishing boats,

talking tour boats,

and many others
to safely pass through.

Terry Turtle gets tired of waiting. Honk, *Honk,* *HONK!*

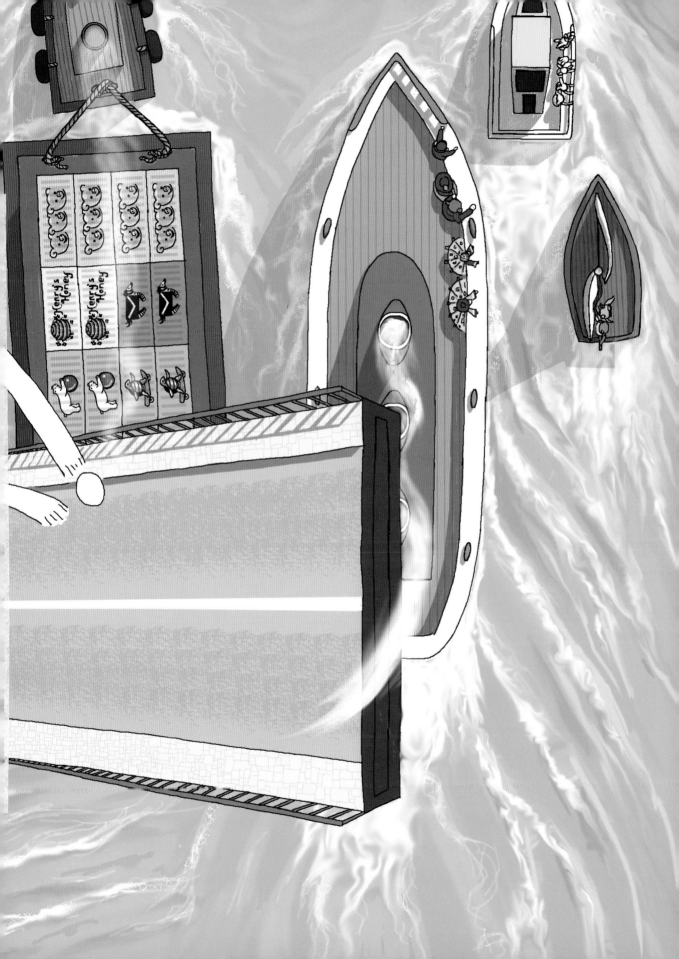

Bridge Tender Todd waves at Captain Josie towing the big barge through the open drawbridge.

He waits until every last boat has passed. Then he can safely close the bridge by reversing the steps – six, five, four, three, two, one.

STEP 6

CLOSE THE BRIDGE. Bridge Tender Todd eases the big lever forward. *Click-brrr-click.*

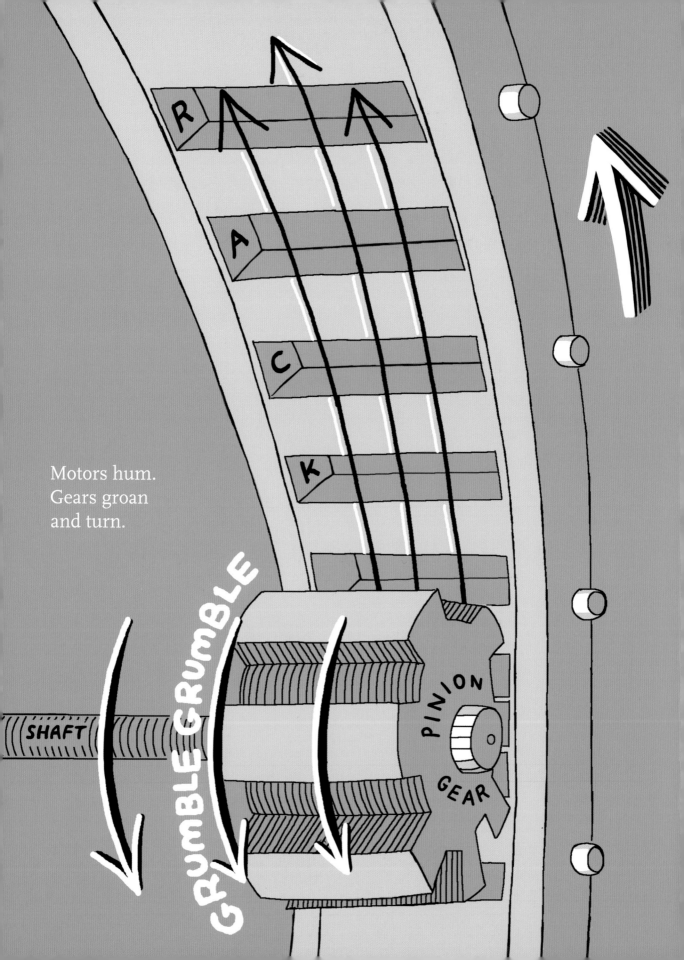

Motors hum.
Gears groan
and turn.

Clang-clang. Flash-flash. Motors hum. Gears spin and whir and slowly the bridge lowers...

down,

down,

down...

to form
a roadway again.

STEP 5

CHECK THE BRIDGE. Bridge Tender Todd looks outside to make sure everything is "A-OK."

STEP 4

LOCK THE BRIDGE. Bridge Tender Todd turns the third switch. Motors hum and metal scrapes as the drawbridge is locked down for street traffic.

CLANG CLANG CLANG

THE NARROWS
DRAWBRIDGE

BUILT ONCE
UPON A TIME
LONG, LONG
AGO BY
THREE PIGS
CONSTRUCTION

STEP 3

DOUBLE CHECK. Always careful, Bridge Tender Todd looks outside. . .

and checks the gauges to make sure the bridge is completely closed and "A-OK."

TRAFFIC GATES. Bridge Tender Todd turns the second switch and the traffic gates go up, up, up. And everyone gets ready to cross the bridge again.

BELLS AND LIGHTS. Bridge Tender Todd turns the first switch. The bells quiet and the lights stop flashing so everyone knows it is now safe to cross the bridge.

Many times each day Bridge Tender Todd opens. . .

and closes the drawbridge. Keeping everyone safe. . .

and happy –
even Ponticat.

AUTHOR'S DEDICATION:
To future bridge tenders, tugboat captains, and bridge builders.

ILLUSTRATOR'S DEDICATION:
To you, dear reader,
I hope that once you reach the end, you will want to begin again.
Special thanks to Mom, Dad, Michael, Ernest,
Ellen Beier, and Susan Wooten.

Werks Series
www.PTMWerks.com

Published by CurlyQPress
www.CurlyQPress.com

Distributed by Applewood Books, Inc.
www.awb.com

ISBN: 978-1-941216-02-6
E-ISBN: 978-1-941216-03-3

Library of Congress Control Number: 2013920649

Printed in China

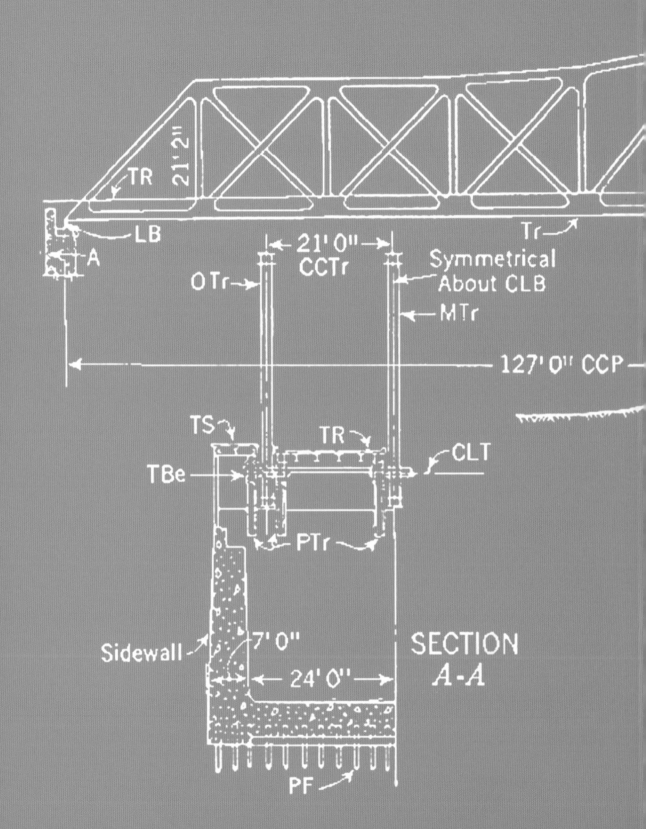

TR
21'2"
LB
A
21'0"
CCTr
OTr
Symmetrical
About CLB
MTr
Tr
127'0" CCP
TS
TR
CLT
TBe
PTr
Sidewall
7'0"
24'0"
SECTION
A-A
PF